CHAPTER 1

Hoggle's Happy Toys

Years ago, children used to peer past the toy factory gates, hoping to spot the wonderful toys inside.

Now they ran past the entrance, scared and trembling. No one would stop there, not even if they were dared.

The children of Cherryville all knew the factory was an evil place. Something awful had happened inside five years ago. It was something kids still whispered about in the playground and used to frighten each other at sleepovers.

Some people said the toys had gone mad. Others suggested that there had been a gruesome teddy-bear mass murder. There was even a theory that the dolls had strangled each other with their hair. None of the children in the town knew the truth for sure. They just knew that they should stay away from that factory.

It was all boarded up with wooden planks nailed across the windows and doors. The tall gates were always kept padlocked. The gold letters painted above the doorway had started to peel and fade, but you could still see they read:

Hoggle's Happy Toys.

But there was nothing happy about these toys.

Some people said that they could sometimes hear dolls whispering in there. Or that they'd seen the shadow of a teddy bear running across one of the windows. But how could this be possible if the factory had been closed down for years?

No one ever said the word "haunted". But nobody wanted to go into the toy factory. And one person who *especially* didn't want to go into the factory was Tess Pipps.

Ten-year-old Tess lived on a farm with her family, and it was a very special farm too. For a start, its cows produced all kinds of flavoured milk, from chocolate to strawberry to banana. The farm's bushes grew sugar mice. And they had lollipop trees and cola-bottle trees and even toffee apple trees!

Tess loved living on the farm, but last month something dreadful had happened – a health-food shop had opened in town. Up till then, the farm had supplied the huge boarding school nearby with its milk and treats, but now the school had cancelled their contract with the Pipps. They'd started ordering carrot juice and

pickled vegetables from the new health-food shop instead.

The boarding school had hundreds of pupils, and they ran a summer school in the holidays. They had been the farm's biggest customer. Now that the school had stopped ordering supplies from the Pipps, whole pails of chocolate milk were going sour and the bags of sugar mice were collecting dust. Tess's mother and father talked about money a lot, and what they could do to save the farm.

Tess loved the cows. She loved their smell and their brown eyes and the way they would push their big heads up against her to say hello. But last night her father had said that they might have to sell some of them.

Tess couldn't bear the idea. The cows were part of the family. They couldn't send them away. They just couldn't. She'd miss them even more now that school had finished for the summer holidays. She opened the kitchen door and found her parents and siblings already sitting around the kitchen table. From the sounds of it, they were in the middle of a very excitable conversation.

Tess's youngest brother, Oliver, gave her a huge grin and said, "Guess what? Dad doesn't have to sell the cows after all!"

"What?" Tess asked, and gaped at Oliver. "Why not?"

"Because the Hoggle's Happy Toys factory is reopening," her father said.

"*What?*" Tess was shocked.

"I'll be able to get employment there," her father went on. "Your older brothers too. There are plenty of jobs going because no one seems to want to work there."

Tess frowned. "Of course they don't. Everyone knows the toys went mad and started killing each other."

Tess's older brothers and father laughed, as if what she'd said was ridiculous. But the younger children didn't laugh. They knew it was true.

"Honestly, Tess, you shouldn't talk such nonsense at your age," her mother said. "Come and sit down and have your dinner."

Tess took her seat at the table and tried to feel pleased about the factory reopening. After all, if it meant that they could keep the cows, then it was a good thing. In fact, it was wonderful. And yet, Tess couldn't squash down the nagging feeling of dread in the pit of her stomach.

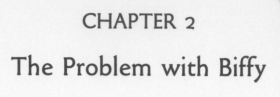

CHAPTER 2

The Problem with Biffy

Unfortunately for the Pipps, their plan didn't quite work. The new owner of the toy factory, Marmaduke J. Hoggle, was only employing children.

"No one knows why," Tess's older brother Mika said to her as she mucked out the cowshed. "But this Hoggle chap insisted on it. He told us, 'No one over twelve.' So you and the younger ones will have to do it."

Tess paused, her shovel in the air. There was a loud splat as some cow dung fell on the floor. "Do what?" she asked.

"Work at the toy factory, of course," Mika replied. "Just for the school holidays. Perhaps a few weekends."

"But I can't!" Tess said. "My place is on the farm."

"Do you want to save the cows or don't you?" Mika asked.

"Of course I do!"

"Well then, you've got no choice," Mika told Tess. "Unless you can think of some other way of earning all that money fast ... Or unless you're too scared of the toys ..." Mika grinned at her in a mocking way.

Tess frowned and leaned the shovel against the wall. "Do you really not remember what happened with Biffy?" she asked.

Mika gave her a strange look. "What are you talking about?"

Biffy had been Mika's childhood teddy bear, purchased from Hoggle's Happy Toys before the factory had closed down. Biffy had been white and fluffy with a small black nose, and Mika had loved him. Until the day Mika ran screaming from his bedroom saying that Biffy had tried to stab him with a fork.

"Biffy attacked you," Tess said as she watched her brother closely. "You cried non-stop for a day. You wouldn't go to sleep until Dad promised to lock Biffy up in the basement. And even then you said you could hear him scratching at the door and rattling the doorknob with his paw all night. The next day, you made Dad throw Biffy away. Surely you haven't forgotten?"

For a long moment, Mika just stared at her. Tess thought she saw his face flicker with a memory. But the next second, Mika threw back his head and roared with laughter.

"You've got a crazy imagination," he said.

Tess crossed her arms over her chest. "Dad laughed at me yesterday too, and yet he's never let us have any Hoggle toys in the house since Biffy."

Mika waved a hand. "Only because Hoggle toys were expensive, Tess. And then the factory closed down anyway."

Tess didn't believe it. Surely the adults must realise that there was something wrong with the toys? Tess could still remember the terror in Mika's scream when he'd run away from Biffy. And she could still remember the suspicious look on her mother's face when she'd looked at the bear. It was as if, deep down, her mother *knew* that there was something not quite right about it.

"Anyway, I've got chores to do," Mika said, interrupting Tess's thoughts. "I can't stand here listening to your teddy stories all day. I'll see you later."

Tess watched Mika go. She knew that she would have to work at the Hoggle's Happy Toys factory. She knew there was no other way to save the farm and the cows that lived on it. But she also knew that she would have to be very, very careful. And watchful. And, most of all, she must make absolutely sure that she did not forget the danger one day, as other children like Mika seemed to do as they grew older.

CHAPTER 3

Meeting Marmaduke J. Hoggle

The next day, Tess and her younger siblings walked to the toy factory. They found the gates wide open, like the factory was waiting for them. It was a creepy sight. The children felt a thrill of dread as they hesitated outside.

Tess could feel Oliver holding on to her coat. The six year old had always been a bit timid, and Tess had to make an effort not to get annoyed with him sometimes. Tess also had eight-year-old twins Niles and Stacy with her. The twins both wore glasses and had dark hair and freckles like Tess. Oliver's hair, on the other hand, was as orange as a carrot and tended to stick up on end.

There had been unease at home before they'd left that morning. Tess's mother hadn't been very happy about them going. But if she'd said something, she'd be admitting that there was something wrong with the factory, that there was something sinister about the toys ... and that was something no adult would ever do. Tess thought that perhaps that was what Mr Marmaduke J. Hoggle was counting on.

There was a sign at the front gates welcoming all job seekers and asking them to report to Mr Hoggle in the factory. The sign had been there for two days, but so far Tess hadn't heard of the factory taking on a single employee. Tess guessed that any adults would have been turned away like her father was. And the other children in the town weren't so desperate for money. But the Pipps kids had a farm to save.

Tess led the others across the deserted concrete yard, kicking aside the odd bit of stray rubbish as she went. They stopped outside the wooden front doors painted with manically grinning toys. The doors were covered in grime and the paint was beginning to peel away in flakes. Tess knocked, but the echoes faded fast and no one answered. She knocked again, more firmly this time.

"Let's go back, Tess," Oliver whispered, tugging at her coat. "I don't like it here. Let's go home—"

"Shut up, Oliver," Tess said, and shook him off. "Do you want Mum and Dad to sell the farm?"

Oliver didn't reply.

"Well? *Does* he want them to sell it?" a voice said from behind them.

The children screamed. Tess whipped round to face a tall man who was looking at the group with vague interest. He was wearing a strange mixture of clothes: a purple top hat that made him seem even taller than he really was; one blue velvet glove and one orange; a white shirt and yellow bow tie beneath a too-big green coat; black trousers and green pointed shoes. Tess saw that his eyes were a pale blue and his hair was a light brown, from what she could see under the hat.

"Who are you?" Tess demanded.

"I'm the toy maker," the tall man replied. "Who are you?"

"We've come to see Mr Hoggle about employment," Tess told him.

"Are you all under twelve?" he asked.

"Yes, but—"

"You're hired."

"Are you Mr Marmaduke J. Hoggle?" Tess checked.

"Yes, I already told you, I'm the toy maker. Marmaduke Jaron Hoggle at your service." He gave them a bow, then said, "You'd better come in. Then you can get right to work."

The children parted to let him past to the door. Everyone held their breath as Hoggle put his velvet-gloved hand on the door handle and pulled it down.

Nothing happened.

Frowning, Hoggle tried it again. He then threw his body hard against the door, making the children jump, but still it didn't open.

"Blast," Hoggle muttered to himself. "Those wretched teddies have locked me out again."

Tess felt three small pairs of hands clutch at her with fright.

"What was that you said?" she asked, trying to keep her voice level. "About the teddies?"

"Hmm? What?" said Hoggle. "Oh, nothing. Don't worry, I have a key in here somewhere."

He produced the key from a pocket. A moment later, Tess heard the groan of a rusty old lock. Hoggle turned back to them with one hand still resting on the door. His voice was almost a whisper as he said, "Are you ready, children?"

Tess heard Oliver and the twins whimper behind her. She was feeling more than a bit afraid herself at the thought of going into the old factory. But it was the only way to save the farm and the dear cows. And Tess had to be brave for the young ones. So she stood up straight and nodded firmly. "Yes," she said. "We're ready."

Hoggle pulled down on the handle, which clicked this time. He pushed the double doors using both of his hands and they swung inwards on creaking hinges. Then he stepped aside, giving Tess and her siblings a perfect view of the large foyer in front of them.

CHAPTER 4

Enter the Factory

The toy factory's entrance was a large circular space. It had a wide spiral staircase twisting up to the floor above and a great crystal chandelier hanging from the centre of the ceiling. Everything was covered in a coat of dust ten centimetres thick, so it was hard to tell what colour things were supposed to be. It was grander than Tess had expected – more like a mansion than a toy factory. It was terribly dirty, but at least there was no blood or teddy-bear hearts lying around.

There were plenty of teddy bears on the walls, however. The entire room was decorated with wallpaper of bears having picnics. They were dressed like people, with lots of top hats and parasols, and Tess thought it was horrid.

"This is the main foyer," Hoggle said as he led the way inside. "As you can see, it's in a frightful mess, so the first thing I want you to do is get it cleaned up. I can't make toys in a dirty factory ... Well, what are you all standing outside for? Come in, come in!"

The children shuffled into the foyer reluctantly, their feet kicking up clouds of dust that made them sneeze.

"There is a map somewhere," Hoggle said. He covered his nose with his hand and moved away from the dust storm. "It's over here, I think. Ah, yes, here it is. Come and have a look."

Tess and the others walked around to the wall behind the large reception desk.

"This is a map of the toy factory," Hoggle said. Tess saw that there were rooms with labels such as "Teddy-Bear Room", "Mermaid Room" and "Dolls' Hair" on them. Hoggle pointed at the map with his blue glove. "It's split into two floors, you see. We're here in the room marked 'Foyer'. And two corridors and the staircase lead off from it. The factory can be a bit confusing, so try to memorise this map if you can. I can't be running around after you the whole time. I've far too much to do. And if you get lost in here, then we might never find you."

Oliver gasped and Hoggle grinned. "I'm joking, of course," Hoggle said. "We'd find you at some point, I expect. Now, there are buckets and mops and dusters and things in the cupboard over there. I want you to clean the factory until it is sparkling. Any questions?"

"When do we get paid?" Tess asked.

Hoggle glanced down at her with a raised eyebrow. "Ah, an entrepreneur."

"What's an entrepreneur?" Tess asked. She was afraid that Hoggle might be insulting her.

"It means a bright, intelligent person who will go far in life and one day make their fortune," Hoggle replied. "You will be paid at the front gates at six o'clock – when it is time for you to go home. Once I have inspected your work and seen that it has been done properly, I will give you your wages myself. And now I shall leave you to get to work and start earning that money."

Hoggle turned and strode from the room, leaving deep footprints in the dust as he went. The children watched him go in glum silence.

"Well," Tess said, trying to sound positive. "Let's get to work."

She led the way over to the cupboard Hoggle had pointed out. When she opened the door, a whole load of mops and brooms fell out on top of them. There were dusters and buckets at the bottom of the cupboard. Stacy squealed because there was a dead spider inside a bucket. Tess told her to not be so silly and throw the spider outside. "If we're expected to clean the whole factory," Tess said, "then there will probably be a lot more dead bugs to come."

But worse than the dead spider was what they found in the last bucket – thirteen small knives, each about the size of a thumb.

"Teddy-bear daggers," Niles whispered.

They all peered at the knives.

"Is there any blood on them?" Stacy asked.

"Don't be daft," Tess told her. "Teddy bears don't bleed."

"Why not?" Oliver said with eyes as big as saucers.

"Because," Tess replied. "They haven't got any blood. They're just full of stuffing."

"Oh. Well ... what should we do with them, Tess?" Niles asked.

Tess thought for a moment. "Throw them out," she said at last. "If Hoggle really is going to start making toys again, then we don't want the new teddies getting any ideas." Tess handed the tiny daggers over to Niles and said, "I saw a rubbish bin out in the yard. Go and put them in there. Oliver, you go with him."

When the two boys came back in, Tess gathered the children close and said, "Now listen – never go anywhere on your own, OK? We move around the factory in pairs. If you need to go to the bathroom, take someone with you. Stay within sight of each other at all times – understand?"

The other children nodded with serious, nervous looks on their faces.

"Right," Tess said, rolling up her sleeves. "Let's get started."

CHAPTER 5

A Terrible Picnic

Tess and the other children spent the whole morning cleaning the foyer. It was dirty, grubby work and nobody enjoyed it.

Tess was scrubbing at a very stubborn bit of mould growing on the base of the reception desk when she heard a long, loud "*Atishoo!*"

She glanced up and said, "Bless you, Oliver."

Her younger brother looked startled. "*I* didn't sneeze," Oliver said. "I thought it was you."

Tess frowned. She could see Niles and Stacy outside emptying a bucket, so it hadn't been one of them. She stood up and stared around the foyer, looking for the phantom sneezer.

"There!" Oliver said as he raised his hand and pointed at the supply cupboard.

Tess was sure she had firmly closed the door, but now it was open a crack. And there on the floor, poking out from behind the door, was a mass of pale yarn that looked very much like doll's hair.

Oliver gave Tess a horrified look. "There's a doll hiding in the cupboard!" he whispered. His lower lip started to tremble. "How did it get there?" Oliver asked.

Tess rolled up her sleeves and marched over. If there was a doll hiding in the cupboard, then Tess would soon drag her out.

But when she threw open the door, she saw that the mass of yarn was just a mop head. There was no sign of a doll or of any other toys in there at all.

"It's just a mop," Tess said, holding it up.

"But then ... who sneezed?" Oliver asked.

Tess gazed around the empty foyer, unable to answer the question. Niles and Stacy walked back in then and asked Tess what they should do next.

Tess sighed and said, "This room is spotless. There's nothing left to clean here, which means we're going to have to move on. Into the factory."

Nobody wanted to do this, of course, but the foyer was as clean as it could be. They had no choice but to set off down one of the corridors with their cleaning supplies.

Tess led the way and saw that the corridor was covered in the same awful teddy-bear-picnic wallpaper as the foyer. There were no windows, but lamps lined the walls, giving everything a sickly sort of glow. She could see several closed doors stretching away from them down the corridor.

Tess was about to walk up to the first door when Stacy let out a squeak and pointed at the wallpaper.

"I know," Tess sighed. "It's very ugly."

"No, look!" Stacy gasped. "Look at what they're eating. Look what's in the sandwiches!"

Tess looked more closely and then sucked in her breath. She hadn't paid much attention to the picnic before, but now she saw what seemed to be dolls' fingers sticking out of the teddy bears' sandwiches. And dolls' eyes in the bowls. There was even a doll's head being used as a ball in some kind of game in the background.

Tess shuddered and then glanced back at the younger ones. "We all knew that the teddy bears were warped and evil before we came here, didn't we?"

Her siblings nodded back, looking miserable.

"Come on, then," Tess said.

They carried on walking, but then something dropped off the wall just in front of Tess. It rolled across the floor until it came to rest against her shoe and stopped. She thought it was a marble at first, but then she picked it up and saw it was a doll's eye. A cold white ball, with a blue iris painted in the middle. The eye even had several thick eyelashes glued to the top.

"What is that?" Oliver demanded.

Tess showed it to him without saying a word. They all jumped as another eye popped right out of the wall, and another and another, until there were dozens of eyes rolling around on the floor.

"They're coming out of the wallpaper!" Stacy cried, pointing.

Tess saw she was right. One of the bowls of eyeballs on the wallpaper was somehow spilling real dolls' eyes out into the corridor.

"But ... that's not possible!" Tess exclaimed. She stared at the wall, feeling cross. Evil, rampaging teddy bears was one thing – she had expected those. But dolls' eyes coming out of the wall was something else altogether and Tess wasn't going to put up with it.

Oliver went to run towards the nearest door, but Tess grabbed his collar and yanked him back. "No!" she snapped. "We stay together."

Oliver whimpered but said nothing. And then the flood of eyeballs stopped as quickly as it had begun and the wallpaper was just innocent drawings once again.

"I can't do this, Tess," Oliver whispered. "Please. Let me go home."

Before Tess could reply, there was another sudden sneeze that made everyone jump.

"*ATISHOO!*"

"Who was that?" Stacy asked. She pushed her glasses further up her nose and stared around wildly.

"There's something in the walls," Tess said as she let go of Oliver and tightened her grip on the mop in case she needed it as a weapon.

The other children gasped and looked worried.

"Do you think it's one of the evil teddy bears?" Niles asked in a low voice.

"I don't know," Tess said, and she narrowed her eyes at the nearby wall. The picnicking teddy bears gazed back at her with what seemed to be challenging looks. Tess thought there was something smug about the bears' whiskers.

She raised her mop and banged on the wall hard with the handle.

"Is something in there?" Tess demanded, trying to sound stronger than she felt.

There was no reply, but one teddy bear in the wallpaper suddenly caught Tess's eye. There was something different about it and Tess realised what it was. The bear didn't have painted eyes like the rest of them. Instead its eyes were holes. It was as if something might be hunched behind the wall, peering out at them unseen ...

Tess lunged forwards before she could lose her nerve, and pressed her face up close to the teddy bear's eye holes. To her horror, Tess saw two pale-yellow eyes staring straight back at her from behind the wall.

She screamed and jumped back, banging into the others, who all started yelling too.

"What is it? What is it?" they cried.

"There's something behind the wall!" Tess gasped.

As if to prove it, the sneeze came loudly once again.

"*Atishoo!*"

There was a scrabbling sound, as if whatever was back there had started to move. It was followed by a flurry of sneezes.

Tess was afraid it might be coming out to get them, so she started banging her mop handle on the wall as hard as she could.

"Get out of here!" she yelled. "Scram! And don't come back or we'll bash you with mops!"

The scurrying sound seemed to get lower, as if the thing was going down underneath the floor. Finally, there was silence and when Tess peered into the eye holes again there was nothing there.

"Is it gone?" Stacy asked, trembling as she gripped Tess's hand.

"I think so," Tess replied, wiping sweat from her brow.

"What was it?" Niles asked. "A teddy bear?"

"I'm not sure," Tess said. "I couldn't see it properly. All I know is it had big yellow eyes."

The children gave each other dark looks.

Then Tess said sharply, "Where's Oliver?"

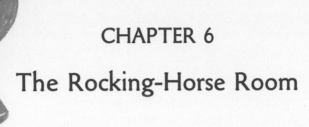

CHAPTER 6

The Rocking-Horse Room

Tess looked frantically up and down the corridor, but her youngest brother was nowhere to be seen.

Niles shook his head and said, "He got scared and ran in there."

He pointed to the nearest door, which was now wide open. Tess scowled and stalked towards it.

"Stupid, stupid!" she muttered. "I told him not to go anywhere by himself. I *told* him!"

The sign on the door read: "Teddy-Bear Room". Tess very much hoped that Oliver hadn't gone inside. It would be just like him to make everything ten times worse.

Tess poked her head into the room and stared at the sight of dozens of teddies. Row upon row of them, all lined up neatly on shelves attached to the walls. They were all identical to Biffy, the bear that had tried to stab Mika – white and fluffy, with black noses and shiny, watchful eyes.

There was a big pile of rusted machinery in the centre of the room. Tess guessed it had been used to make teddy bears.

"Oliver!" Tess called. "Oliver, it's all right! You can come out!"

But there was still no sign of him, and no reply.

"Perhaps he's hiding behind the machinery," Tess said, thinking out loud.

She strode into the room and poked around the machinery from every angle, as well as underneath, but there was no Oliver.

Tess looked back at Niles and said, "Are you sure he came into this room?"

"I don't know," Niles said. He pushed his glasses up his nose and looked unsure. "I *thought* it was this one. And the door was open …"

Niles trailed off and Tess groaned aloud. "I can't believe he ran off like that!" she said. She suddenly felt both angry and worried at the same time.

"He can't have gone far," Tess said. She was trying to reassure herself as much as the other two. "We'll just have to search for him."

Tess walked back over to the twins, fighting to control the panic rising inside her. It was her fault that Oliver was lost. She was responsible for him and now he was gone.

"The bears," Stacy said, pointing at them and staring. "They're completely clean."

Tess realised Stacy was right. The floor of the room was as dirty as the foyer had been, and the machinery was covered in rust. But the white bears were spotless, as if they'd been made yesterday.

"Perhaps Hoggle only just made these ones," Tess said.

But it seemed like an awful lot of bears to have produced so fast. And the machine in the centre looked as if it hadn't been used in years.

"Never mind about the bears," Tess said, shaking her head. "The important thing right now is to find Oliver. He must have gone into one of the other rooms."

They returned to the corridor and hurried back to the foyer to see if he had gone that way, but there was no sign of him.

"Perhaps he ran home?" Stacy suggested.

"But I really thought I saw him go into the Teddy-Bear Room," Niles said.

Tess clenched her hands into fists and tried to think.

Maybe Oliver *had* simply run off home. It sounded like the sort of dumb thing he'd do. On the other hand, perhaps he was lost somewhere inside the factory. Teddy bears could be stabbing Oliver with forks at this very minute!

Finally, Tess looked at the twins and said, "Someone should run home to check if he's there. Stacy, you're the fastest. You go and then come back to tell us."

Stacy nodded, her face serious. "I'll run as fast as I can," she promised.

Tess and Niles watched Stacy whizz out of the front doors. She sprinted down the drive and past the entrance gates, kicking up clouds of dust behind her. Then Niles and Tess returned to the corridor. They had put down most of their cleaning stuff, but Tess kept hold of the mop, as it was the closest thing they had to a weapon. They went to the next door in the corridor, which had a sign glued to it that read: "Rocking-Horse Room".

Tess had never been too fussed about dolls and teddy bears, even when she was small. But she had always adored rocking horses. Her family had never been able to afford to buy her one, but whenever she'd seen a rocking horse in a toy shop, she'd pressed her nose up against the window longingly.

Tess opened the door and she and Niles walked into another large room, with grey light coming in through the dirty windows. Tess couldn't prevent herself from gasping. Inside were some of the most beautiful rocking horses she'd ever seen. They were all different colours, with real hair for their manes and tails. Some of the horses leaned against the wall, half finished, while others were scattered around the floor. They all had proper saddles and reins made from leather.

But the strange thing about the rocking horses was that they all looked terrified. Some of them had wide, staring eyes, as if they'd just seen something dreadful. Other horses had flaring nostrils or open mouths. One horse in particular caught Tess's eye and she walked over to it.

Most of the horses were brown or black or dappled grey, but this one was white, with a golden mane and pink ribbons in its tail. It had a silver twisted pole in the middle and reminded Tess of the horses she'd seen on fairground carousels.

"You're beautiful," Tess breathed.

Like all the others, this horse had a wild, desperate look on its painted face. Tess slowly reached her hand out to stroke its nose. Her

hand rested there for a moment as she looked into the horse's frightened eyes.

And then the horse snorted into her hand. Tess felt the warm puff of its breath against her skin. Niles heard it and let out a yelp behind her, then shouted a warning. But Tess didn't think the horse meant to hurt her. In fact, there was a look in its eye that seemed almost ... pleading.

"Tess, let's go," Niles said. "We know these horses are evil, and Oliver isn't here."

Tess turned away from the white horse reluctantly. She was halfway back to the door when there was a soft whinny behind her. The kind of sound she'd heard real horses make in the fields around their farm. Tess turned back towards the white rocking horse and saw that its face had changed. It now looked more heartbroken than scared and Tess felt guilt twist in her stomach.

"Let's go!" Niles said again.

Tess joined her brother and they walked out of the Rocking-Horse Room.

"Maybe it's not what we thought," Tess said as she closed the door behind them. "Those horses didn't seem evil. They just seemed scared."

She glanced at the horrible wallpaper of the teddy bears' picnic and thought about what they'd done to the dolls.

"We know the bears are dangerous," Tess went on, remembering Biffy. "But perhaps the other toys aren't like them?"

Niles shrugged. "Who cares?" he said. "I hate this place. The sooner we find Oliver, the sooner we can leave."

Tess didn't say anything more, but the encounter with the rocking horses had got her thinking.

She and Niles started to make their way down the corridor to the room next door. Then they heard the sound of whistling. Something was coming towards them from the corridor up ahead – and it was getting closer.

CHAPTER 7

A Buffalo Hunt

Tess tightened her grip on the mop. The whistling sounded loud, so whatever it was must be big. Tess's mind filled with visions of giant teddy bears that could squeeze the life right out of her with one evil cuddle.

But there was no time to hide, because it was almost upon them. Tess shoved Niles behind her, stood firm and raised the mop, ready to strike.

But it was only Hoggle who charged around the corner. He was still wearing his large green coat, purple top hat and mismatched gloves, but now he also gripped a stick with a huge net hanging from the end of it. It looked like a butterfly net but was much, much bigger.

Hoggle stopped whistling when he saw them and came to an abrupt halt. For a moment he looked startled, but then he said, "Ah, yes, the children. Good day to you." He tipped his top hat. "Excellent job in the foyer."

Tess stared at the net in Hoggle's hand. "What's that for?" she asked, pointing.

"This?" Hoggle asked. He held up the net and gazed at it. For a moment, he was silent, but then he said, "Just a spot of dragonfly hunting, my dear."

"But that net's big enough to capture a ... a buffalo!"

It wasn't *quite* large enough for a buffalo, but it was a very big net just the same – almost as large as Hoggle himself.

"Not many buffalo herds around here that I'm aware of," Hoggle said cheerfully. "No, I think I'll stick to dragonflies." He looked at them again and said, "Weren't there more of you small people this morning?"

"Our brother, Oliver, went into the—" Niles began, but Tess cut him off.

"Oliver and Stacy are cleaning a different part of the factory," Tess said firmly. She was afraid that if Hoggle knew that Oliver had vanished, then he might not let them stay in the factory – and then they'd never find their brother. Oliver would become nothing more than a sad memory.

Tess found herself wondering just how much Hoggle *did* know about the toys. Surely he must have known there was *something* strange about them or else he wouldn't be walking around the factory with a gigantic net. Whatever Hoggle had said, Tess was pretty sure he wasn't really hunting for dragonflies.

"Mr Hoggle, I was just wondering," Tess said, "was the man who built this factory a relation of yours?"

"Yes, indeed," Hoggle replied. "Caractacus Hoggle was my grandfather."

"People around here tell stories about the factory, you know," Tess said.

"Do they now?" Hoggle replied.

"Yes." Tess nodded. "They say that Caractacus Hoggle went mad and started making evil toys."

"Well, well," Hoggle said.

"Do you think it's true?" Tess pressed.

"Do *I* think it's true?" Hoggle repeated. He paused, then said, "After my grandpops closed the factory and moved back home, he used to tell me the most dreadful stories about this place. I thought he'd just lost his marbles a bit. The Hoggle family are prone to losing their marbles, you know." Hoggle scratched his neck and said, "When I inherited the factory, I thought I'd come and take a look for myself."

"And what do you think now?" Tess asked.

Hoggle adjusted his top hat and said, "You ask an awful lot of questions, small girl. And I'm not paying you to ask questions. I'm paying you to scare away ... that is to say, I'm paying you to clean the place."

"You were about to say something else then!" Tess exclaimed.

"No, no," Hoggle said. "Just a moment of confusion, that's all."

"What are you hoping we'll scare away?" Tess demanded.

Before Hoggle could answer, there was another sneeze from inside the wall.

"*Atishoo!*"

"What is that thing in the wall?" Tess asked.

"What thing?" Hoggle replied.

"That thing that just sneezed!"

"I didn't hear any sneeze," Hoggle said.

Tess narrowed her eyes at him. Why was he lying?

"You know there's something wrong with the teddy bears, don't you?" Tess said. "Adults can't normally tell, but if you didn't know, then you wouldn't have said about them locking you out of the factory earlier."

"My dear," Hoggle replied. "Please be assured that there is no need to worry about the teddy bears. There are none left in the factory."

Tess opened her mouth to argue, but Hoggle held up a gloved hand to silence her.

"This morning was my mistake, I admit," Hoggle said. "I thought I had got rid of all of them, but it turns out there was one left. I found it while you were cleaning the foyer."

"But ... but we've been in the Teddy-Bear Room since then," Tess said. "And it was full of teddy bears. Dozens of them!"

Hoggle gave Tess a startled look, then shook himself and said, "Not possible."

"I tell you we saw them!" Tess exclaimed. She was starting to feel cross. "Come and look if you don't believe me."

Hoggle followed them back down the corridor, where Tess threw open the door to the Teddy-Bear Room.

"See!" Tess said triumphantly. "I told you."

"Tess!" Niles said. He was tugging at her sleeve, but she ignored him.

Hoggle looked over her head into the room. "Just as I thought," he said. "Not so much as a whisker."

"*What?*" Tess said.

Tess spun around and stared into the room. Hoggle was right. There wasn't a single teddy bear in sight. Nothing but row upon row of empty shelves.

"But they were there!" she said. "Just a few minutes ago!"

"Children have such wonderful imaginations," Hoggle commented. "Simply marvellous." He glanced down at Tess and said, "Still, imagination is not all that helpful in employees. My own fault for hiring children in the first place, I suppose."

"Why *do* you only hire children?" Tess asked.

Hoggle shrugged. "Why not?" he replied. "You'd only be wasting your time in school otherwise. Now, I must get on." He waved the net. "I've dragonflies to outwit and you two have rooms to clean."

And, with that, Hoggle set off down the corridor, whistling to himself once again. Tess and Niles watched him go, while wondering how on earth a roomful of teddies could have simply vanished.

CHAPTER 8

The Mermaid Room

Tess was just thinking that it would be hard for things to get much worse when Stacy suddenly came sprinting down the corridor. Tess could tell from her sister's face that it was not good news.

"Oliver isn't there!" Stacy gasped, skidding to a stop. "At home, I mean!" She bent over, still panting for breath. "No one's seen him all day."

"So he's still here in the factory then," Tess said.

She closed her eyes for a brief moment. She had been so afraid that something like this would happen. She should have listened to her instinct. She should have refused to bring her younger siblings here. But it was too late to change that now.

Tess opened her eyes. The twins were both staring up at her, waiting for her to tell them what to do. She couldn't fall apart.

"We just have to find Oliver, that's all," Tess said. "And then we'll leave. And we won't come back, no matter what. We'll just have to find some other way to save the farm."

And so they continued to explore the factory. First they found a room full of bright yellow rubber ducks that squeaked at them in a panicky sort of way. Then they passed on to a room of jack-in-the-boxes, where they could hear the dolls inside the boxes whispering and weeping to themselves and rapping their knuckles against the wood.

Unfortunately, Niles knocked his foot against a jack-in-the-box as they left the room and it popped open all on its own. A boy doll with a shock of orange hair jumped out, grinning at them wildly as it bounced around on its spring.

Stacy began to wail. "It's Oliver!" she cried, pointing. "They've turned him into a toy!"

"Don't be daft!" Tess exclaimed, and yet she felt a jerk of unease deep down.

The jack-in-the-box *did* look a bit like Oliver, with its orange hair and big green eyes ...

Tess shook her head firmly. "This toy is really old," she said. She stuffed the doll back in the box and closed the lid with a snap. "Look how dusty it is. It can't possibly be Oliver."

Still, Tess felt deeply troubled as they left the room. After all, this was no ordinary factory and the normal rules didn't apply here. What if children *could* be turned into toys?

The idea was too dreadful to think about and Tess pushed it from her mind as they opened the next door. They found themselves in a room that was almost empty apart from some toy soldiers and a few mermaid dolls.

Stacy adored mermaids and had pictures of them painted all over her walls back at home.

She forgot her fear of the toys, exclaimed in delight and ran straight over to the mermaids. Their hair was made from blue and green yarn that hung all the way down their backs, so long they could sit on it. And they wore shell jewellery and had sparkly, shimmering scales on their tails.

Tess and Niles joined Stacy and looked at the mermaids on their shelf. They were all slumped together in a dusty heap, as if they'd been there a long time. There was something unloved and forgotten and sad about them. Stacy reached out and began to straighten them up.

Tess was about to warn her against touching the mermaids when suddenly the air filled with the scent of the sea. The children all gasped. They had only been to the seaside once, when their parents had taken them on a special holiday a few years ago. But they all remembered the wonderful smell – a mixture of salt and shells and seaweed.

For a moment, Tess almost thought she could hear the roar of the surf and feel the warm sand against her toes.

"Can you smell it too?" Niles asked.

Before anyone could reply, one of the mermaids moved her painted lips and spoke.

"Will you help us?" the mermaid said in a soft voice. "Please?"

The children jumped. Tess grabbed her younger siblings by the arms and pulled them back a few steps. But the mermaids made no move towards them. In fact, they didn't move at all, apart from their lips.

"Oh, please," another mermaid whispered. "Please help us."

This mermaid was still lying down and her face wasn't pointed towards the children. Tess expected her to turn her head, but she stayed lying on the shelf.

"Can't ... can't you move?" Tess asked. She took a cautious step forwards.

"Only the teddy bears can move," the mermaid replied. "The rest of us can only talk."

Tess slowly reached out and propped the mermaid up against the wall. The air still smelled of the sea, and Tess could almost taste salt on her lips.

"How can we help you?" Tess asked.

"Get rid of the teddy bears," one of the mermaids said in a trembling voice. "They hate all the other toys. The first toy maker locked the teddy bears up in a box, but then this new one came and let them all out. They've already killed the baby dolls. They'll come for the rest of us next."

"Why are they so evil?" Stacy asked. "How did they get this way?"

"We don't know," the mermaid said. "One day we all just came to life. The teddies have been evil since then."

"Have you seen our brother?" Tess asked. "He's about this tall." She held her hand out flat above the ground. "And his hair is as orange as a carrot. You can't miss him."

"We haven't seen him," the mermaids replied. "But if he's lost in the factory, then the teddy bears have probably taken him."

"Taken him where?" Tess demanded, feeling panic rise up inside her once again. "They won't … they won't turn him into a toy, will they?"

Tess couldn't help thinking of that jack-in-the-box that had looked so much like Oliver.

"They'll take him to the tunnels," the mermaid said.

"What tunnels?"

"There's a whole network of tunnels underneath the factory. It's how the teddy bears move around."

"How do we get to them?" Tess asked eagerly.

"You can't. The entrance is behind a locked door. And only the toy maker has the key."

CHAPTER 9

The Secret Diary

The children promised to come back for the mermaids, but first they needed to find Oliver. They tore around the rest of the factory and finally found the locked door. It was big and heavy and made of wood, and there was no way they were getting past it without the key.

"The mermaids said Hoggle has it," Tess said. "Perhaps it's in his office."

She glanced back down the hallway. A few minutes ago they had passed a door with a frosted glass window with gold words that read: "Toy Maker's Office".

They hurried back down the corridor only to find that this door was locked too.

"I bet Hoggle has the key on him somewhere," Tess said. She turned to her siblings. "None of us are pickpockets – we'll never be able to snatch it from him." Tess looked back at the door. "So we're just going to have to break the window."

"I know!" Niles said. "There was a Noah's Ark Room just down there. We can use one of the arks."

They went back to fetch one of the large wooden boats and then Tess hurled it at the window with all her might.

Fortunately, the glass was old and delicate. It shattered immediately.

Being careful to avoid the broken shards, Tess reached in and twisted the door handle from the inside.

"We've got to be fast!" Tess whispered. "Hoggle might have heard the smash. Everyone look for a key."

They slipped into the room, which had a great big desk in the middle and lots of bookcases lining the walls. Stacy and Niles went to the bookcases and Tess investigated the desk. She yanked open the drawers and rifled through them.

"What's this?" Tess said, pulling out a big heavy book.

It was bound in red leather and had Caractacus Hoggle's name on the front. When Tess opened it, she realised it was a diary. A page had been marked with a paperclip and the diary fell open to this.

Tess's eyes went to a highlighted paragraph of small, neat handwriting. She skimmed over it and then gestured to the others.

"Listen to this," Tess said, and then started to read aloud from the diary:

Today I ventured down into the tunnels once again and pleaded with the goblin, but he will not undo the magic spell placed on the toys. The teddy bears continue to rampage around the factory, destroying everything in their path. To my dismay, some of the bears had already been sold to families. I visited these homes and it was plain to me that the children were terrified of the teddies. But most of the adults seemed to think me perfectly mad when I tried to warn them about the toys. Oh, there were one or two adults who seemed to sense something was wrong and had already thrown the toys away, but their unease seemed vague – just that something wasn't quite right.

Most of the adults had no idea at all. There was one mother who threatened to telephone the asylum when I tried to explain. And a father who seemed blind to one of the teddies running about his living room and brandishing a knife in the most savage manner. I can only assume it is part of the goblin's magic that adults don't see the toys come to life.

But when an adult is inside the factory itself, they see and hear all. Several of my best workers have already walked out, vowing never to work with toys again. They didn't even wait for their wages! And there are rumours and whispers in the town about strange sights and sounds coming from this place.

Oh, how I wish I'd never set eyes on that goblin, let alone thrown pennies into the wishing well! All I ever wanted was to create extraordinary toys, but that fiendish goblin granted my wish in the most twisted manner imaginable. I cannot risk making new toys. Not with that vile goblin's magic poisoning the entire factory.

I fear I have no choice but to close the place. My life's work is in ruins ...

Tess trailed off. Then she said, "He goes on about his life's work being in ruins for a bit after that." She flicked back to the start of the journal and scanned the pages rapidly. "It looks like he discovered a wishing well in a cave while out on a country walk," Tess told the other two. "So he built his toy factory on top of the wishing well on purpose – in order to keep the wishing goblin to himself." She shook her head. "Stupid thing to do," she tutted. "The goblin didn't like having his home built on and so he granted the toy maker's wish with an evil twist. When Caractacus Hoggle wished for his toys to come to life, the goblin made the bears wicked. But only children can see it. Adults are normally clueless."

Stacy and Niles stared at Tess with wide eyes.

"The goblin must have been the sneeze we heard," Niles said in a low voice. "In the walls. The thing with the yellow eyes."

Stacy and Tess nodded. Everyone knew that goblins were allergic to children.

"I bet that's why Hoggle is hiring kids," Tess said. "To scare the goblin away. He almost said as much earlier."

"So now we have an angry goblin to deal with as well as mad teddy bears," Stacy said.

The children gave each other grim looks.

"Well, come on," Tess said. "We still need to find this key. Oliver is depending on us."

They tore around the room, very aware that Hoggle himself might return at any moment. Tess was just beginning to despair that they might never find the key when Stacy gave a shout of triumph from across the room.

"Here it is!" Stacy exclaimed. "It was hidden inside the giant atlas."

"Well done!" Tess said, and hurried over to take the big brass key from Stacy. It felt cold and heavy in Tess's hand as she curled her fingers around it.

The children returned to the locked door and everyone held their breath as Tess inserted the key.

There was a soft *click* as she turned it and the door swung slowly open. They saw a staircase leading straight down to a dark, silent basement. Tess peered into the gloom and then glanced back at the twins, who'd both gone pale.

And Tess knew that she couldn't take them with her down there. Not after what had happened to Oliver. She couldn't risk losing Stacy and Niles too. She had to get them out of harm's way. But she knew they wouldn't simply agree to abandon her to the darkness and the evil teddy bears. So Tess thought carefully about what to say next.

Finally, she said, "I need you two to go outside and stand guard."

"Outside?" Niles repeated, wrinkling his nose. "But—"

"I saw Hoggle walk off down the road from the window in his office," Tess lied. "So I need you two to stand at the front gates and keep watch for him. If Hoggle comes back, then one of you can keep him talking while the other one comes to warn me."

The twins hesitated, but Tess said, "I *really* need you to do this. It's very important that Hoggle doesn't discover me down there." She glanced back towards the basement.

"All right," Stacy said at last. "We'll stand watch."

"Good," Tess replied. "And if I'm not back in an hour, then I want you to go straight home and tell Mum and Dad what's happened. *Make* them believe you. OK?"

"But you will come back, won't you?" Niles said, looking scared. "With Oliver?"

Tess tightened her grip on the mop. "Yes," she said. "I'll come back with Oliver. But there's no time to lose, so you two go outside and I'll see you soon."

The twins gave Tess a quick hug before leaving her alone.

Tess turned back to the open doorway and gazed at the stone staircase leading into the darkness. Her hand already ached from holding onto the mop so tightly.

"Don't worry, Oliver," Tess whispered. "I'm coming."

CHAPTER 10

The Goblin's Lair

Tess's heart was thumping so loudly in her chest as she went down the spiral stairs that she felt sure the goblin would be able to hear it. The stone walls were wet and there was a damp, musty smell in the air.

She had to go slowly to allow her eyes time to adapt to the dark. But as she got nearer the bottom, a greenish glow spilled out of the darkness towards her. And the smell of damp gave way to the scent of goblin, which was something like black pepper and toffee apples mixed up together.

Finally, Tess reached the end of the staircase and found herself in a long tunnel. She knew at once that the goblin lived down here, because the tunnel was lined with goblin candles. Goblins made them from their bogies, so they were a yucky green colour. And the candle flame burned green too. The light made Tess feel like she was in some kind of underwater swamp. She could even hear the trickle of running water from somewhere.

Tess *really* didn't want to be in the tunnel, and part of her longed to run straight back up the stairs and all the way home to the farm. But she had to find her brother first.

"Oliver?" Tess called softly.

There was no reply and she didn't dare shout louder in case the goblin heard her. So she swallowed down her fear and made her way deeper into the tunnel. As the mermaids had told them, there was a network of tunnels that spread out under the factory. Sometimes the path Tess was on would branch off into a cavern or cave, and it wasn't long before Tess feared she was lost.

Finally, she turned into another tunnel and realised that there was something else at the end of it, just around the corner. She could see its shadow against the wall. And it was too big to be Oliver.

The goblin! Tess thought to herself.

Before she could lose her nerve, Tess crept right up to the corner, then leaped around it and flung out her mop.

There was a pained cry and a thump, and something big fell down on the floor before her.

But it wasn't the goblin – it was Hoggle lying on the ground. His top hat had fallen off and he dropped his enormous net to grasp his nose with both hands.

"Aargh!" Hoggle groaned between his fingers. "My nose! I think you may have broken it!"

Tess wasn't in a very sympathetic mood just then. She pointed the mop at Hoggle sternly and said, "It's no good pretending any

more – we've seen your grandfather's journal and we know everything! We know there's a goblin down here and that he's making the teddy bears evil! We know that—"

"Yes, yes, it's all true!" Hoggle exclaimed, cutting Tess off. He looked up at her with pleading eyes and said, "But how was I to know? I thought Grandpops had just gone round the twist when he went on about those bears. Like him, I've always wanted to make toys."

Hoggle dropped his hands. Tess was relieved to see that his nose wasn't bleeding and didn't seem to be broken.

Hoggle waved his arms about from where he was half-propped on the floor and said, "I wanted to make the most wonderful, fantastic, amazing toys that children would love for ever! Is that so bad?"

"No," Tess said, starting to feel uncertain.

Hoggle gave a great sigh and said, "When I found out about the goblin, I thought hiring children would chase him away. I can't have adults here – they'd be able to see there was something wrong with the toys. When the teddies are out in the world, the magic hides their evil from adults for the most part – although some adults seem to realise something's not right. I thought that once you children had chased away the goblin, then the factory could have a fresh start."

"Well, it was a very risky scheme!" Tess said. "My brother Oliver has vanished! Perhaps the teddy bears have him, or perhaps it's the goblin. Whatever it is, I've got to find him."

"Good gracious me!" Hoggle breathed. He'd gone pale as he stared up at Tess. "I'm so sorry," he said. "I really did think that the teddy bears were all gone. I locked them all in a cupboard but they must have escaped. And

I never dreamed the goblin would take a child. Not with the goblin's allergy to children—"

Right at that moment, there was a sudden loud, "*ATISHOO!*"

It came from further down the tunnel. Hoggle and Tess stared at each other for a moment, then Hoggle scrambled to his feet and the two of them sprinted towards the sneeze.

Tess and Hoggle rounded the corner and found themselves in a particularly large cave, with stalactites reaching down from the ceiling and big chunks of crystals set in the walls. In the centre of the space was a small wonky well made from chipped red bricks. It didn't look like anything that special, but Tess knew it must be the wishing well, because the goblin was crouched on its wall. The scent of black pepper and toffee apples filled the air.

The goblin was completely green, with arms and legs like a frog's, webbed fingers and ears

that seemed far too big for him. He was about
the size of a small sheepdog and crouched
on the edge of the well. As Tess watched, the
goblin reached down and pulled something
up from the depths. A shock of orange hair
appeared and Tess gasped as she realised the
goblin was dragging Oliver up by his collar.

Oliver grabbed the wall of the well and pulled himself onto it. His face was streaked with dirt, but otherwise he seemed OK. Tess gave a cry of relief and ran towards him, just as Hoggle raised his net and charged towards the goblin.

"Unhand that child, you monster!" Hoggle cried.

The goblin jumped, startled, and whipped around to face them.

Tess saw huge frightened yellow eyes before Hoggle brought his net down and scooped the goblin up.

"Well done!" Tess cried, delighted. She threw her arms around Oliver. "Are you all right?" Tess asked.

But, to her surprise, Oliver wriggled out of her hug and ran up to Hoggle.

"Let Betty go!" Oliver yelled, poking Hoggle hard in the ribs. When that didn't work, Oliver grabbed Hoggle's arm and bit him on the hand. Hoggle dropped the net with a shout.

"Good heavens!" Hoggle exclaimed. "I've always liked children very much indeed, but I do wish you'd all stop jabbing me and biting me and hitting me with mops!"

"Oliver, what's wrong?" Tess asked. "Who's Betty?"

"The goblin!" Oliver replied, hurrying over to the net where the goblin was still thrashing about. "She's not evil. Betty saved me from the teddy bears and let me hide in her wishing well. She was going to take me home."

Oliver reached into the net and grasped the goblin's hand to pull her out. Tess watched with shock as the goblin shrank against Oliver and wrapped her webbed hands tight around his leg. Betty's head only just came up to Oliver's waist.

"Is this true?" Hoggle asked, staring at the goblin. "Did you save the boy?"

The goblin hesitated, then nodded. Tess noticed that Betty had extremely long eyelashes.

"But … aren't you in league with the teddy bears?" Tess asked.

"Me?" the goblin said. Her voice was cold and soft, like ice cream. Betty pointed a finger at Hoggle and said, "*He's* the one who made the bears!"

"I most certainly did not!" Hoggle exclaimed, sounding offended. "My grandfather made them. Then he threw a penny into your well and wished for his toys to come to life."

"It wasn't *my* wishing well back then!" the goblin protested. "It was my uncle's."

"Well, where is your uncle?" Hoggle asked.

"He died," the goblin replied. "A few weeks ago. He left me the well. I thought this would make a lovely new home, but then I discovered the place was infested with evil teddy bears." Betty gave a loud sniff and her lower lip wobbled slightly. "And I've got nowhere else to go."

"Ah," Hoggle said, and he rubbed the tip of his nose. "I think there has been a misunderstanding."

CHAPTER 11

A Very Special Penny

Tess was glad to learn that the goblin wasn't in league with the teddy bears, and nor was Hoggle. In fact, it seemed as if everyone wanted the same thing.

"We must get rid of these bears," Hoggle said, sounding fed up. "I keep thinking I've found them all and locked them away. And the next thing I know they've popped back up and are running around the factory again. The teddy bears must have secret hiding places. Even the teddies on the wallpaper make rude faces and gestures at me."

"Some of my uncle's magic must have gone into the wallpaper," Betty said. She stuck a bony finger up her nose, pulled a bogey out and ate it.

"What?" Betty said as she noticed their expressions. "Picking my nose is the only thing that will ward off the sneezes." She turned to Hoggle and said, "The bears can pick the lock of that cupboard you keep putting them in. And they hide themselves away in the underwater streams that go beneath the tunnels." She pointed at the back of the cavern. "The streams start there."

Tess thought about the frightened mermaid dolls and was struck with an idea.

"I think I know what we need to do!" Tess said. She turned to the goblin and asked, "Can you grant wishes like your uncle?"

Betty nodded. "If you throw a penny into the well," she replied.

"The mermaid dolls told us that the other toys can only talk – they can't move around like the bears," Tess said. "The mermaids also said that the bears hate all the other toys and have been attacking them. So what if you bring the rest of the toys to life, Betty? I'm sure they would help us round up the teddy bears. The mermaids and rubber ducks would be able to dig out any bears that try to hide in the streams. The teddies would be outnumbered."

Betty pulled out another bogey, flicked it into her mouth and chewed thoughtfully. "Actually," she said. "That's a pretty good idea."

*

Tess and Oliver went to fetch Niles and Stacy in from outside. The twins were introduced to the goblin and told about everything Oliver and Tess had discovered. Then Betty got back in her wishing well and Hoggle stood ready with a penny to throw in.

They'd agreed Hoggle would give the children a head-start of five minutes so they could grab some sacks from the storage cupboard. Then they were to run into the various rooms and warn the toys about what was going to happen and the plan they'd made to capture the teddy bears.

The children ran around the rooms as fast as they could, talking to the toys. They spoke to the rubber ducks, the jack-in-the-boxes, the Noah's arks, the toy soldiers and the mermaid dolls. The mermaids wept with relief and promised that they would go straight to the streams to round up the teddies.

Finally, the children reached the Rocking-Horse Room. When Tess opened the door, she saw that the white horse she'd spoken to before still looked heartbroken. Tess hurried over to it and whispered their plan into its ear.

And she was just in time. Hoggle must have thrown his penny into the well and made his wish, because sparkling gold ribbons seemed to fill the room, wrapping around the horses. They could smell the marzipan scent of magic as it fizzed and popped in the air.

Suddenly the rocking horses were coming to life all around them. They tossed their heads and swished their tails and stamped their hooves against their rockers. The white horse nuzzled its soft nose against Tess's neck, snorting into her hair with joy. Its eyes no longer looked sad and scared but bright and happy instead.

"It worked!" Tess exclaimed. She turned to her siblings and said, "Niles and Stacy, collect as many mermaid dolls and rubber ducks as you can and carry them down to the stream in the goblin's cavern. It will take them too long to get there without any water to travel on. Oliver and I are going to help the toys up here."

The twins hurried off. Tess was about to stride towards the door to lead the horses out when the white horse gripped her sleeve between its teeth and gave a gentle tug. When Tess looked back at it, the horse tossed its head towards its saddle. Tess realised that the rocking horse wanted a rider, and she grinned and leaped straight onto its back.

Oliver took Tess's lead and scrambled onto a dappled grey horse that whickered to greet him.

"Let's go!" Tess cried.

The horses leaped from their rockers and galloped out of the door into the corridor.

Tess saw that the toy soldiers were already ripping down the teddy-bear wallpaper. The painted bears were throwing dolls' eyes at the soldiers, but they easily ducked them.

And the real teddy bears were being driven out too. When they reached the foyer, Tess saw a small group of them racing across the floor,

chased by some wooden elephants from the Noah's arks. The bears looked just like Biffy and were running as fast as their fluffy white legs could carry them. But they weren't fast enough and Tess's horse galloped straight to them. Tess reached down and scooped them up in her sack. The bears wriggled and grumbled but could do nothing to escape.

It was the same all over the factory. Everywhere the teddy bears went they were confronted with dolls or toy animals or soldiers or the Pipps children. When the bears tried to escape into the streams, the mermaids and rubber ducks soon got them back out again.

Finally, everyone had gathered back in the foyer to stare down at four big sacks full of wriggling teddy bears.

"Marvellous!" Hoggle exclaimed, rubbing his hands together with glee. "Is that all of them, captain?"

Hoggle was speaking to one of the toy soldiers, who stood to attention and said, "Yes, sir, that's the lot. We've gone around the entire factory and there are no bears left."

"At last," Hoggle said.

"You need to put them back in your grandfather's trunk," Betty said, and she gave the sacks a wary look. "It's got a padlock attached on the outside, so they won't be able to pick it from in there."

"I'll put them straight in," Hoggle said with a nod. He smiled at the goblin and said, "That was a marvellous job you did, bringing those toys to life. Simply marvellous." He adjusted his top hat and added, "Perhaps you and I could be partners, Betty? With your magic and my craftsmanship, I have a feeling that Betty and Hoggle's Toy Factory would make the most wonderful toys the world has ever seen. We'd share the profits, of course."

Betty gave Hoggle a wide grin and shook his hand. "It's a deal," she said.

"This has been a real adventure, but we should be going," Tess said, glancing towards the windows. It was getting dark outside and she knew that her mother would be starting to worry about them.

"I must fetch your wages first," Hoggle said. "After all, you've worked hard, even though it was at a different job than you'd thought."

"Do you think there might still be jobs for us here?" Tess asked hopefully. "It's just that we really do need the money to save our farm. And you'll need people to help if you're going to start making toys again, won't you?"

"Indeed, yes," Hoggle replied, looking pleased. "If you'd like to come back at the same time tomorrow, I'm sure I'll find jobs for you."

"Oh, thank you!" Tess said. She was thinking of the cows back home and that perhaps they might be able to save them after all. "Well, we'll see you tomorrow, then—"

"Wait a moment," Hoggle said. "I owe you four a great deal." He looked thoughtful and rubbed his chin. "In fact, I think you have all earned a special bonus. How about a toy each to take home?"

The children gasped.

"To keep?" Stacy squealed.

"Absolutely," Hoggle replied. "You may each pick one toy."

"Oh, I'd just love one of the mermaid dolls!" Stacy said.

"I'd like a toy soldier!" Niles cried.

"Can I take Betty?" Oliver asked, looking longingly at the goblin.

"Betty isn't a toy," Tess said, and tutted at Oliver. "Plus you just heard that she's going to be Hoggle's new partner."

"Perhaps you could come to our house for tea, then?" Oliver suggested to Betty.

The goblin pulled another bogey from her nose and inspected it on the end of her finger. "Would your parents mind?" Betty asked.

"Perhaps we could meet you in the woods for a picnic instead," Tess said.

"Well, if I can't have Betty, then I'll have a rubber duck," Oliver announced.

"Say please," Tess said.

"Please."

"And you?" Hoggle asked, turning his bright blue eyes on Tess. "What would you like?"

Before Tess could even reply, the white rocking horse was whinnying and tugging at her sleeve.

Hoggle grinned. "It looks as if the toy has already chosen you," he said.

Tess threw her arms around the rocking horse. Even though the toy was made of wood, the scent of real horses and sweet hay seemed to fill her nose.

"Thank you, Mr Hoggle," Tess said. "I promise we'll take good care of them."

CHAPTER 12

The Teddy-Bear Heart

The children were on their way home from the factory when Tess said, "Remember Dad's rule about Hoggle toys? He might not let us have them in the house. I think we should keep our toys a secret for now."

"How?" Stacy asked, and she clutched her mermaid doll to her chest. "Mum will probably be looking out for us from the window. She's bound to see your horse."

The white rocking horse neighed and nudged Tess gently.

"I know," Tess said. "We'll go round the back and hide the toys in the cowshed for now. We can smuggle them into the house later."

So they did just that – finding a warm corner of the cowshed for the toys to nestle down for the night.

Then the children went around to the front door of the house where their mother was waiting for them on the doorstep.

"Oh, there you are!" she exclaimed, hurrying forwards to greet them. "You had me worried."

"There was a lot of cleaning to do, Mum," Tess said. "We didn't realise it was so late."

"Mr Hoggle should have made sure that you left on time," their mother said, sounding annoyed. But then she smiled at them and said, "Well, you won't have to go back anyway. I heard there was an absolute riot at the summer school when they tried to serve the health-food shop's carrot juice and pickled vegetables. So the school won't be using them any more and have re-ordered our chocolate milk and sugar mice."

"They have?" Tess gasped.

Her mother nodded, beaming. "Yes, they've already paid us up front for the next year. So, you see, you won't need to work at that toy factory after all."

Tess glanced at her siblings, who all looked crestfallen.

"Actually, Mum," Tess said, turning back to her. "We all really enjoyed it there today. And Mr Hoggle says he needs a lot of help to get the factory started up again. Perhaps we could carry on working there? Just for a bit?"

Their mother stared at them. "Gosh, that was a turnaround!" she exclaimed. "This morning you hated the idea. Well, I suppose we can spare you for a couple of days. Now come on in and have some dinner."

Their mother led the way inside, but Tess paused on the doorstep and heard the faint whinny of a small white rocking horse from the cowshed.

"Goodnight, toys," Tess said softly. "We'll come back for you tomorrow."

Then she turned and followed her family into the warm glow of the farmhouse.

*

Meanwhile, the toys in the factory were having a celebration. They weren't just free of the evil teddies who'd made their lives such misery, but they could finally move around on their own too. It seemed fitting to have a party, with much music and laughter and dancing.

Hoggle had given them a record player, and a blue mermaid and a silver mermaid were taking it in turns to select new records.

The silver mermaid was fussing over a small red object. "What's that?" the blue mermaid asked.

"This?" The silver mermaid looked up with a guilty expression. "Oh, it's a teddy-bear heart."

"*What?*" The blue mermaid was horrified. "Where did it come from?"

"One of the teddies gave it to me in the stream," the silver mermaid said. "Just before he was rounded up."

"You should have thrown it away!" the blue mermaid said.

"I was going to. But then … I found that I couldn't. It's so pretty."

"It could be dangerous," the blue mermaid told her. "Let me see it—"

But the silver mermaid pulled it away. "The teddy gave it to me, not you!" she said, sounding alarmed. "He said you might all be jealous and try to take it from me. He said there was only one way to keep it safe."

And the silver mermaid stuffed the small heart straight into her mouth and swallowed it whole.

The blue mermaid gave a shout of dismay. "You shouldn't have done that!"

"Ooh! Perhaps you're right!" the silver mermaid replied. "It's awfully strange to feel it beating in there." She pressed a hand to her chest. "And there are all these odd thoughts in my head."

"What kind of thoughts?" the blue mermaid demanded.

"Well, for a start," the silver mermaid said, staring at her. "I never noticed how long our hair was before. Have you? I used to look at my hair and just think how pretty it was. But now when I look at it, all I can think is …"

"What?"

"That it's long enough to *strangle* someone with!" the silver mermaid exclaimed with glee.

"Oh," the blue mermaid said. "I *really* don't think you should have swallowed that heart!"

Before the silver mermaid could reply, the door banged open. Hoggle cartwheeled into the room, barely containing his excitement.

"Well, well," he said, rubbing his hands. "What incredible and extraordinary toys we are going to make here now that the last traces of bad magic are gone!"

The toys cheered and clapped. All except for the two mermaids who simply looked at one another. The silver mermaid knew she should speak up and tell Hoggle what had happened. But instead she found herself glaring at the blue mermaid and hissing out words in a frightening voice that hardly sounded like her own.

"Don't even think about telling Hoggle about the heart!" she said to the blue mermaid. "You'll be sorry if you do!"

The blue mermaid gave her a scared look and gulped. But she didn't say a word and the silver mermaid breathed a sigh of relief.

She had got away with it.

Nobody suspected a thing.

Our books are tested
for children and young people by
children and young people.

Thanks to everyone who consulted on
a manuscript for their time and effort in
helping us to make our books better
for our readers.